♥ IREAD
皮皮與波西：恐怖大怪獸

繪　　　圖	阿克賽爾‧薛弗勒
譯　　　者	酪梨壽司
責任編輯	倪若喬
美術編輯	蔡季吟

發 行 人	劉振強
出 版 者	三民書局股份有限公司
地　　　址	臺北市復興北路 386 號 (復北門市)
	臺北市重慶南路一段 61 號 (重南門市)
電　　　話	(02)25006600
網　　　址	三民網路書店 https://www.sanmin.com.tw

出版日期	初版四刷 2020 年 2 月
書籍編號	S858131
I S B N	978-957-14-6108-3

Originally published in the English language as PIP AND POSY:
THE SCARY MONSTER
Text Copyright © Nosy Crow 2011
Illustration Copyright © Axel Scheffler 2011
Copyright licensed by Nosy Crow Ltd.
Chinese translation right © 2016 San Min Book Co., Ltd.

皮皮與波西

恐怖大怪獸

阿克賽爾・薛弗勒／圖　　酪梨壽司／譯

三民書局

下(ㄒㄧㄚˋ)雨(ㄩˇ)了(ㄌㄜ)，
獨(ㄉㄨˊ)自(ㄗˋ)在(ㄗㄞˋ)家(ㄐㄧㄚ)的(ㄉㄜ)波(ㄅㄛ)西(ㄒㄧ)有(ㄧㄡˇ)點(ㄉㄧㄢˇ)無(ㄨˊ)聊(ㄌㄧㄠˊ)。

她_{ㄊㄚ}決_{ㄐㄩㄝˊ}定_{ㄉㄧㄥˋ}動_{ㄉㄨㄥˋ}手_{ㄕㄡˇ}做_{ㄗㄨㄛˋ}點_{ㄉㄧㄢˇ}吃_ㄔ的_{ㄉㄜ˙}。

她走進廚房，穿上圍裙，
把手洗乾淨。

她先拿出

砂糖

奶油

麵粉和雞蛋。

然後將所有材料攪拌在一起。

她把拌好的麵糊裝進模型。

再將烤盤送進烤箱。

小心，波西！
很燙喔！

就在波西等蛋糕出爐時，
忽然聽到拍打窗戶的聲音。

窗外出現一隻毛茸茸的大手！

波西有點害怕。
到底是誰的手呢？

緊接著又傳來敲門聲！

門外傳來一聲：「吼！」

波_{ㄅㄛ}西_{ㄒㄧ}真_{ㄓㄣ}的_{ㄉㄜ}好_{ㄏㄠ}害_{ㄏㄞ}怕_{ㄆㄚ}。

這時門打開了。是一隻大怪獸！
怪獸大吼一聲：「哇嗚！」

波西嚇哭了。

喔，天啊！

大ㄉㄚˋ怪ㄍㄨㄞˋ獸ㄕㄡˋ走ㄗㄡˇ進ㄐㄧㄣˋ屋ㄨ子ㄗ。

波西看到怪獸的腳，
馬上不哭了。

她說：「哈囉，
皮皮！」

皮皮說：「哈囉，波西！
對不起，嚇到妳了。」

「妳想不想當怪獸？」

波(ㄅㄛ)西(ㄒㄧ)穿(ㄔㄨㄢ)上(ㄕㄤ)怪(ㄍㄨㄞ)獸(ㄕㄡ)服(ㄈㄨ)。

波(ㄅㄛ)西(ㄒㄧ)大(ㄉㄚˋ)吼(ㄏㄡˇ):「哇(ㄨㄚ)嗚(ㄨ)！」
皮(ㄆㄧˊ)皮(ㄆㄧˊ)笑(ㄒㄧㄠˋ)了(ㄌㄜ˙)起(ㄑㄧˇ)來(ㄌㄞˊ)。

皮皮和波西到院子裡玩耍，

一直玩到點心時間。

他們喝了牛奶，
還吃了好多蛋糕。

太棒啦！

It was a rainy day and Posy was a little bit bored.

She decided to do some cooking.

In the kitchen, Posy put on her apron and washed her hands.

First, she took out

the sugar   the butter

the flour and the eggs.

Then she stirred everything together.

She plopped the mixture
into the paper cases.

Then she put the tin
into the oven.

Careful, Posy.
It's hot!

Posy was waiting for the cakes
to bake when she heard a tap
at the window.

It was a big, **furry** hand!

Posy felt a little bit scared.
Whose hand was it?

Next, there was a knock on the door!

"Grrr!" said a voice.

Posy was very scared indeed.

The door opened. It was a monster!
"RAAAAA!" said the monster.

Posy started to cry.
Oh dear!

The monster came right
into the house.

But then Posy looked at the monster's feet.
She stopped crying.

"Hello, Pip,"
she said.

"Hello, Posy," said Pip.
"I'm sorry if I scared you.

Would *you* like to be
a monster now?"

Posy put on the costume.

"Raaa!" said Posy.
Pip laughed.

Pip and Posy went out into the garden

and played until tea-time.

Then they had a glass of milk,
and lots of cakes!

Hooray!

繪者簡介

阿克賽爾・薛弗勒　Axel Scheffler

1957年出生於德國漢堡市，25歲時前往英國就讀巴斯藝術學院。他的插畫風格幽默又不失優雅，最著名的當屬《古飛樂》(Gruffalo) 系列作品，不僅榮獲英國多項繪本大獎，譯作超過40種語言，還曾改編為動畫，深受全球觀眾喜愛，是世界知名的繪本作家。薛弗勒現居英國，持續創作中。

譯者簡介

酪梨壽司

畢業於新聞系，擔任媒體記者數年後，前往紐約攻讀企管碩士，回臺後曾任職外商公司行銷部門。婚後旅居日本東京，目前是全職媽媽兼自由撰稿人，出沒於臉書專頁「酪梨壽司」與個人部落格「酪梨壽司的日記」。